Dear Parent:
Your child's love of reading sta........

Every child learns to read in a different way and at his or her own speed. Some go back and forth between reading levels and read favorite books again and again. Others read through each level in order. You can help your young reader improve and become more confident by encouraging his or her own interests and abilities. From books your child reads with you to the first books he or she reads alone, there are I Can Read Books for every stage of reading:

SHARED READING
Basic language, word repetition, and whimsical illustrations, ideal for sharing with your emergent reader

BEGINNING READING
Short sentences, familiar words, and simple concepts for children eager to read on their own

READING WITH HELP
Engaging stories, longer sentences, and language play for developing readers

READING ALONE
Complex plots, challenging vocabulary, and high-interest topics for the independent reader

ADVANCED READING
Short paragraphs, chapters, and exciting themes for the perfect bridge to chapter books

I Can Read Books have introduced children to the joy of reading since 1957. Featuring award-winning authors and illustrators and a fabulous cast of beloved characters, I Can Read Books set the standard for beginning readers.

A lifetime of discovery begins with the magical words **"I Can Read!"**

Visit www.icanread.com for information
on enriching your child's reading experience.

HarperCollins®, 🐱®, and I Can Read Book® are trademarks of HarperCollins Publishers Inc.

Ice Age 2: Geyser Blast!
Ice Age 2 The Meltdown™ and © 2006 Twentieth Century Fox Film Corporation. All rights reserved.
Printed in the United States of America.
No part of this book may be used or reproduced in any manner whatsoever without written permission except in
the case of brief quotations embodied in critical articles and reviews.
For information address HarperCollins Children's Books,
a division of HarperCollins Publishers, 1350 Avenue of the Americas, New York, NY 10019.
www.icanread.com
Library of Congress catalog card number: 2005934815
ISBN-10: 0-06-083968-6 — ISBN-13: 978-0-06-083968-0
Book design by John Sazaklis
❖
First Edition

I Can Read!

READING 2 WITH HELP

ICE AGE 2™ THE MELTDOWN

GEYSER BLAST!

Adapted by Ellie O'Ryan
Illustrated by Artful Doodlers, UK

HarperCollins*Publishers*

Welcome to the Ice Age—
a time when the world was frozen.
Many animals lived on the ice,
like Manny and his friends
Sid and Diego.

One day, Manny saw something strange.

The ice was melting.

"It is going to flood!" he yelled.

Soon their home would be covered

with water.

Sid suggested becoming water creatures.

"Genius," Diego said, rolling his eyes.

But Sid had a point—land animals

cannot live in an underwater world.

It was time to find a new home—fast.

The friends heard about a giant boat.
It was really far away, but it would
take them to dry land.
Manny, Sid, and Diego decided
to travel in search of the boat.

Along the way, they met Ellie
and her brothers, Crash and Eddie.
The group did not all get along at first.
But they soon realized that it would
take teamwork to get where they all
were going.

Look! Diego saw the boat.

Everyone cheered.

The gang would be saved, and
they had gotten there together.

As the group celebrated their journey,
a geyser exploded nearby.
Sid was not worried, though.
"It is just a little water and steam.
How bad could it be?" Sid asked.

Just then a dodo bird sat near Sid.

Whoosh—a geyser blew under the bird!

Boiling water and steam shot
into the sky.

Feathers flew everywhere.

Good-bye, dodo!

Now Sid was worried.

The pressure was too much for Eddie.

"I am too young to die!" he screamed.

"Actually, possums do not
live very long," Crash replied.
"So you're kind of due."
"Ahhhhhh!" wailed Eddie.

Finally, Ellie stepped in to

calm her brothers down.

"Nobody is going to die!" Ellie said.

Manny looked around.

He did not see Ellie anywhere.

Then he looked up.

Ellie was sitting in a tree!

From up there, she saw that the geysers

were spouting in a pattern.

She had an idea.

"I can tell you which way to go!"
she said.

"No way," Manny replied.

He did not want to leave Ellie behind.

There must be another way, he thought.

But there was no other way.

"Mammoths are brave," Ellie said.

"Are you brave enough to trust me?"

"Yes," Manny replied.

He picked up Crash, Eddie, and Sid,

and put them on his back.

Then they made a run for it!

Ellie told her friends where to go.

"Left! Left! Straight!

Right! Straight! Right!

STOP!"

They made it!

"You are home free!" yelled Ellie.

But then a new problem showed itself.

One by one, more geysers erupted.

They were heading straight for

Ellie's tree!

Wham!

A geyser blew up the tree Ellie
was perched in.

Where did she go?

The friends thought the worst.

Then they saw a wonderful sight—

Ellie running for safety.

Crash and Eddie ran to meet her.

Oh, no!

More geysers blew.

The ground split in two!

Manny tried to run to Ellie.

But there was too much steam
and smoke.

Manny could barely see anything.

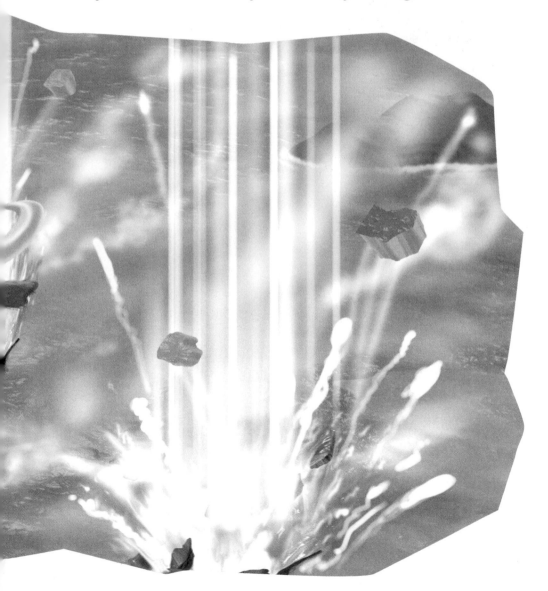

The split in the ground grew bigger.

Manny tried to jump over it—

but Diego stopped him just in time!

Finally, the geysers stopped blowing,

the crack stopped growing,

and the steam started to fade.

Sid opened his eyes.

"Are we dead?" he asked.

No—they were fine!

Where are Ellie, Crash, and Eddie?

Manny wondered.

"ELLIE!" he yelled.

Everyone waited for her to yell back.

"We are okay, too!" Ellie called.

She was on the other side of the crack.

Everyone cheered!

"We will meet you at the boat!"

Manny yelled.

Manny, Sid, and Diego went one way.

Ellie, Crash, and Eddie went
the other way.

"The worst is behind us,"
Manny declared.

On to the giant boat!